CW00643483

ATTICUS

- A Novel -

Juno Jakob

Foreword by Dr. Thomas Richardson

ATTICUS
a novel by Juno Jakob

This hardback edition first published in Great Britain in 2022 by Beercott Books.

Main text © Juno Jakob 2022

Foreword © Dr. Thomas Richardson 2022

Cover design © Beercott Books 2022

Cover fox illustration © Nazaré Prévost 2022

Image opposite © Ryan Maesen 2022

Design & layout © Beercott Books 2022

ISBN 978-1-9163953-9-8

A catalogue record of this book is available from the British Library.

Beercott Books
www.beercottbooks.co.uk

For:

Paige
(for helping me guide my literary kin)

Aaron and Victoria
(for saving my life)

&

John Katzenbach
(for being a friend, mentor & therapist)

Contents

Foreword

Psychosis is a term used to describe mental health problems such as those linked to a diagnosis of schizophrenia. Psychosis is usually characterised by delusions: Strongly held beliefs that others do not share. These are often persecutory in nature, with individuals fearful that they are at risk, that others are trying to harm them, for example being afraid that they are being spied on. Individuals can also experience hallucinations, sensory experiences which other people do not experience, which can be highly distressing. These are often auditory, such as hearing voices, but can also be visual or in other senses such as taste or touch. Those with psychosis can also struggle with what is termed 'negative symptoms' such as difficulty with organising their thoughts and behaviours, low energy, and poor motivation. If frequent and distressing, these can cause problems for example with relationships, work, and socialising.

It is hard for someone who has not experienced psychosis to know what it is like. If you have not heard a threatening voice, it is difficult to know just how real that can feel, how terrifying it can be. I am a clinician who has worked with people experiencing psychosis for several years, I am an academic who has researched psychosis, but I have not personally experienced it. I do not truly know how it feels. I can explain to my students what the symptoms are, but there is only so much understanding you can get from reading a textbook: Personal experiences and stories are so important to really appreciate what it might be like.

In this book Juno paints a vivid and emotional picture of

what it is like to live with psychosis. The frequent visual hallucinations that can be both terrifying and also comforting and supportive. The intrusiveness and intensity of the voices. As I read this book, I really felt I stepped into Dylan's shoes and had some idea of how confusing and frightening it must be to have voices shouting all kinds of abuse at you, the guilt and shame that comes with it. How difficult it can be to be fully open and honest about the symptoms you are experiencing, even with people who care about you, even with people you trust. *Atticus* beautifully and brutally outlines how paranoia, in this case about witches, can escalate and take over ones thinking and have a huge impact on day-to-day life and behaviour to the point that this becomes a person's reality; it is all they can think about. The desperation to keep safe and escape from these experiences is clear in these pages.

Research into the best treatment for psychosis continues, but is making great progress. As well as medication options, there are an increasing number of psychological therapies which target the specific mechanisms which lead to psychosis. Cognitive Behavioural Therapy (CBT) has been shown to reduce distress and help people to cope better with psychosis, and may even delay or prevent psychosis in those who are high risk. These techniques cannot stop the voices, but rather help the person make sense of their experiences and consequently reduce the grip they have over an individual's behaviour. *Atticus* describes some of the techniques that can be used in CBT such as mindfulness, and ways to limit the incessant worrying and ruminating which escalates a small doubt about someone's intentions into an intense and rigid belief that you are at harm.

I was Juno's therapist and worked with him on and off for a couple of years. As a therapist, what I like about *Atticus* is that it describes how therapy for psychosis can be really helpful, but also how difficult it can be; what hard work it is. Unfortunately, many people who start therapy with psychosis don't finish for this reason. The importance of the therapeutic relationship really leaps off the page in this novel; how difficult it is for Dylan to be honest with his therapist about his hallucinations and paranoia. How the voices comment directly on the therapy process. As therapists, I hope *Atticus* helps us understand why therapy can be so hard for those with psychosis, why it can be so difficult to trust mental health professionals.

For those who have not experienced psychosis, I hope that this book gives and insight into what it can be like. I hope it helps you understand, rather than viewing those suffering as frightening and dangerous. They may feel frightened and in danger; this does not mean they are themselves dangerous. For those who have lived experience as a service user or carer with psychosis, I hope that this book talks to your experiences and validates how scary it can be.

I want to thank you Juno for asking me to write this foreword, and commend him for his bravery in discussing his experiences in this semi-autobiographical novel. *Atticus*, built from his own experiences, explains the lived experience of psychosis better than I ever could.

Dr. Thomas Richardson
Associate Professor of Clinical Psychology
University of Southampton, UK

ATTICUS

October 2008

451.
Four hundred and fifty-one.
There were four hundred and fifty-one tiles on the ceiling of
the Raven ward dayroom at St. John's Psychiatric Hospital.

Dylan Samuel, clinically insane, stared up at the ceiling.

He had counted the characterless tiles four times since morning medication as he tried to keep his unsettled mind occupied. Other patients around him on the ward spoke in private conversations, some with other people, some to themselves, but mostly to psychiatric ghosts.

The head 'nurse', whose name Dylan couldn't recall, despite seeing her every day, only looked up from her computer occasionally to eye the crazy folk.

Above her head, Dylan could see the clock ticking high out of reach.

One-twenty-three in the afternoon. Time moves slowly within the hospital walls. The natural laws of science didn't apply in St. John's.

Dylan looked down at his feet to the sleeping fox.

Atticus was the name of the fox for that was the name he had given himself. He was a small fox, no bigger than a timid house cat. He had bright orange fur and silky black feet. Piercing his skull was a sharp arrow, shot through the back of the animal's head and violently through his right cheek. He had crimson blood on his muzzle and nose, but the blood never hit the linoleum floor.

Looking at the pale walls, Dylan was filled with a sting of anger and loneliness. They were plain and boring, nothing to excite the senses but he supposed that the idea was to keep the patients calm and docile.

18

A 'nurse' came out of the locked door next to the 'nurse's' station and looked down at the papers in her hand as she walked into the day room. She walked in a way only the sane can: a mix of authority and purpose. She was a witch, hiding her occult powers.

Atticus perked his ears as if he knew something was happening, but he didn't open his bright amber eyes.

"Dylan?" the nurse called to no-one in particular, without looking up from the papers. "Are you ready to see Dr. Romero?"

> *She's talking to you!*
> *Fucker!*
> *Cunt!*

The voices in his ear roared obscenities.

Rita, as her magic plastic name ID read, gestured to follow. She led Dylan to the locked door and with a swipe of her key opened the door then led them down the long fluorescent-lit corridor lined with the same motivational posters and repetitive artwork that adored every hospital corridor. The walk made Dylan seasick. Bright lights, straight lines and no windows to see the horizon.

No escape.

His legs were heavy and stiff, a side effect from that morning's medication.

The witch named Rita turned occasionally to the patient to make sure he was still following her and gave him the same plastic smile he was sure she gave to every patient on the ward she felt pity for. It seemed to Dylan that Rita, if in fact that was her real name, had a diabolical plan for him and would take pleasure in his pain and suffering.

The timid fox stayed close to his feet, keeping low to the ground.

She's leading you to her Satan's shrine!
Run!
Hide!

Dylan shook his head trying to scatter the voices with his eyes focused on the repeating pattern of the blank carpet.

'Rita' stopped at a closed door as did Dylan and the wounded fox.

"The doctor is waiting for you," she said, not looking up at him, hiding her evil eyes so he wouldn't suspect her, but Dylan knew exactly what she was. The voices simply confirmed his suspicions.

After hesitation, Dylan opened the door.

Dr. Francis Romero stood from behind his desk.

Dylan had thought, at their first meeting nearly two weeks ago, that Dr. Romero reminded him of an old schoolteacher that he had once had, though their face and name had been lost to time and Dylan was left only with the knowledge that the teacher had been kind and nurturing.

The doctor had a dark bushy beard and short hair of the same colour with a few delicate flecks of grey. He was no older than thirty-five, although there was no way of knowing for sure. Dr. Romero did, at least, have a smile that put Dylan at ease.

Today, the doctor wore a white, short sleeve shirt with tiny orange diamonds printed on it. A button was missing about halfway down the shirt which seems to have fallen off since it was worn last week. His blue jeans were scuffed at the knee a little. His brown boots were worn at the toes, making the toes a lighter colour than the rest of the shoe. Like the 'nurse' named 'Rita', he also had a magic card hanging from the shirt's breast pocket.

It was important to note all of the doctor's details in case the witches replaced him with a fraud.

The doctor held out his hand.

He thinks you're a fuckin' parasite!
Suck his cock!
Faggot!

How Dylan wished the voices would silence.

Reaching out his own nervous hand, Dylan shook the doctor's firm grip. There was some abstract level of trust in the action.

"How are you doing today?" Dr. Romero asked.

"I'm okay, Dr. Romero."

"Call me Francis, please," the doctor said, with that kind smile.

Dylan nodded once and looked around the office, recalibrating his memory.

The office was nicer than the Raven ward day room. There was at least some character to this room: a desk piled high with papers and books, a giant plastic fern plant in the corner, a canvas picture of a jazz musician playing a saxophone, two chairs facing each other in the middle of the room and a large window wall that gave a view to the autumn trees outside, gently swaying in the soft breeze.

The plague of black and red beetles was festering under the jazz canvas. Dylan couldn't take his eyes off them. They rolled and climbed over and across each other, clicking their pincers and fighting over rancid, rotting meat.

Francis noticed and followed Dylan's gaze. "Are you okay?"

Dylan's mind stood blank of everything except the beetles, but he nodded an automated response.

The doctor picked up a notebook from the cluttered desk and pointed to the chairs. "Please sit, whichever chair you prefer."

During their first two sessions, Francis had made Dylan sit in the chair with its back to the window, so he was not blocking the space between the doctor and the door. A standard measure in a psychiatric hospital he had been told. Dylan chose the chair facing the window so he could see autumn through a window with no chicken wire mesh in the glass.

Francis began making notes.

It was the same every time Dylan saw a doctor or a psychiatrist. The feeling of uncertainty and exposure. The thought of lying naked on a rack of torture before a doctor to be prodded and poked was unpleasant, but Francis, so far, had made the ordeal bearable with his laid-back approach and manners. Dylan was leaning to the conclusion that Francis wasn't involved in witchcraft but hadn't been able to decide for certain.

"Great, so let's begin," the psychiatrist started, clearing his throat. "So, how have things been?"

"I think...I think I'm doing okay."

"That's good, real good. Now, I know this is our sixth session, but how are you finding them so far?"

Dylan thought of the previous doctor, the one who admitted him and ran the hospital, Dr. Grierson, and remembered how clinical and cold the session and admission to hospital had been. He had felt like an unhappy lab rat.

Churning over his answer in his head, Dylan replied. "Yes, I like them."

"Excellent, that's good to hear," Francis replied, taking a quick glance down at his notebook as he jotted down a sentence. "How are you finding the ward?"

"It's okay. Slow some days and a little cold but I have my bath robe," Dylan explained.

"Are you keeping busy?"

"I try to."

"Last time you mentioned your writing. How's that going?"

"I'm not finished yet."

"Finished? What are you writing?"

"A short story."

"About?"

Dylan shifted in his chair. "I don't like to say until it's finished."

23

Francis gave an understanding look and held up his hand. "That's fine. Maybe one day I'll be able to read your work."

You're a fuckin shit writer!
Worthless ramblings of a madman!
Dumb, thick cunt!

"One day," Dylan replied, trying to ignore the inner voices.

Silence, except a distant cry on the ward.

The doctor must have seen it was a dead end. "So...you're feeling okay. Good."

"Okay...just worried."

Atticus yawned and wandered the room, avoiding the ever-growing pile of beetles. It was a comfort seeing the fox. Dylan had come to accept him as a pet of sorts. A silver lining in mental illness.

"What are you worried about?" asked the doctor, moving slightly forward in his chair.

Dylan instantly felt under pressure.

Faggot!
He's going to fuck you raw!
Hit him! Hit him now!

Today, the voices were oddly monotone and flat. Closing his eyes, Dylan tried to quiet them. He hated when they talked like that. They said vile things. Disgusting, vulgar things. Sometimes, when he was stuck in a cold and dark place, they spoke so loud he could barely hear what was happening in the real world around him. They were a constant, horrid white noise in his ear. Never silencing. Never relenting. They were always stealing Dylan's thoughts and implanting filthy new ones. Things that made him sick to his stomach and head... but he couldn't help but hear them.

"...okay?"

Dylan opened his eyes to a concerned looking Francis and the voices went quiet to a murmur.

"Are you okay?" Francis repeated.

Nodding, Dylan came back to the room.

"I was asking, what do you think you're worried about?"

"I don't know... lots of things... lots of things."

The psychiatrist made a quick note and looked at his troubled patient. "Lots of things, you say. Do you remember me mentioning worry periods last session?"

"Mmm hmm," mumbled Dylan, though he was unsure if he did indeed remember.

"Where we take time out of our day to sit and face our worries. Be it alone or with someone. Talking about our worries helps us see them for what they really are," Francis explained methodically.

Dylan noticed, for the first time, that the doctor had a small scar on his upper lip where his beard didn't quite grow properly.

Another detail the witches couldn't copy.

"So, our worries can sometimes become bigger worries because we fester on them," Francis held up his pen. "For instance, what do you think would happen if I dropped my pen? What's the worst thing you can imagine happening?"

Starting at the gold-coloured fountain pen, Dylan felt his mind nearly burst at the fragile seams. Suddenly, no thought was still, and his mind was racing full speed ahead of him. The horrible familiar sensation that he was not thinking anything for himself returned. It was as if he was merely watching someone unseen, no doubt a witch, switching stations on a television with a hidden remote. He couldn't grasp a solid thought long enough to process it. Ideas, memories and fears flew by too quickly, like driving at speed through an unfamiliar town with only vague glimpses of dark buildings and faces. Like thunder from the heavens, the people in his ear roared with turmoil. Dylan vigorously shook his head, feeling his brain move inside his skull with such force it felt like a sucker punch from a powerful, heavyweight boxer. A burning urge to be outside washed over him. He felt he needed the cool breeze on his face and an open space to wash him free of confusion.

Dylan stood and swayed from the headrush. "I…"

"Hey, hey, Dylan. It's all okay. We're just talking things through slowly. We don't need to talk about anything you don't want to," Francis assured.

Dylan sat slowly, his mind coming back to normal speed.

"I was asking about worry periods," Francis said after a few moments of needed quiet.

"Yes… I remember… kinda… then pens."

Francis held up his pen again. "Yes, so what do you think the worst thing that might happen is if I dropped my pen on the floor?"

Dylan turned the thought and question over in his mind carefully, as if he were handling a delicate object with a gentle but firm grasp.

He began slowly, trying to not mumble. "It could… crack the ground… spill ink… then it would get damp… the carpet would be ruined… it would get mouldy… and that attracts… bugs…"

There was a knot of dread as he spoke the last word out loud.

The doctor made a note. "Can you see how we went from a simple little pen dropping onto the floor to a situation with mould and bugs? Now, that might be a possible scenario, but I very much doubt it. Your mind has made a leap to link what appears to be a very serious fear of yours: bugs."

Real or not. Hallucination or reality. Dylan hated bugs.

"What we need to try and do is take a step back, remember? Try and imagine ourselves stepping back from a big painting and try to focus on the bigger picture instead of small details. Like we discussed last week, we need to step back and look logically at the steps our minds have taken," said Francis.

"But...but what if you can't think logically?" Dylan countered.

"Well," Francis began, seeming to pick his words carefully. "I suppose that's why we're here. We're here to help you get to the point where you CAN start thinking logically again and challenge the strange thinking you struggle with. To get you back in touch with reality again. I know that sounds difficult and daunting but, as they say, the hard things in life are the things worth doing."

Dylan agreed, somewhat, with the statement and silence fell over the room once again. He tried to think clearly but the fog was too thick.

"I don't... know..." replied Dylan after a minute of reflection. "I find it difficult. I find it hard to separate thoughts sometimes. It's all a kind of... big..."

Searching his mental vocabulary, he found only simple words appearing in his head as if waiting to be said; Cat, Pen, Water, Book. Dig.

Dig?

Like dig a grave.

The witches planted that word, he was sure. They would make him dig his own grave before they bewitched him and ate his corpse.

"It's all a big lump," Dylan said, not sure if his mind was on the right track. The shadow of gravedigging lingered behind his eyes.

"The lump might be easier if we can try and break it down into smaller pieces," Francis suggested.

"Maybe."

"So, let's take one problem or thought, just a small section at a time."

It was getting frustrating trying to single out one thought.

Over the years, Dylan had decided on a filing system of sorts for his mind. He called them 'Boxes'. There were boxes for everything and in his mind's eye the boxes were stacked in a grand old library from some forgotten time. Inside, every aisle of the library had its subject and every subject had multiple boxes. There were boxes for memories, boxes for facts and lessons he had learnt, boxes for books he had read, boxes for childhood pets and school day crushes. Just about anything Dylan had experienced in life had a box. The fear boxes were hidden in the back of the library where Dylan hoped and prayed they would stay shut. But, along with trying to find places for each of those memories and thoughts, there was also the maintenance of the boxes and over the last few months, the boxes had begun to tear and fade as if damp and weathered. Some thoughts were starting to bleed into each other, overlapping different ideas and mysteries that were unknown. Suddenly, a very pleasant memory of his best friends, Maya Fox and Henry Crane's engagement party the previous summer was now scarred with images of a violent car crash he had witnessed when he was fourteen years old. Memories of his grandmother in Brighton and happy times he had had in the town were now marred with the painful memory of him breaking his arm when he fell from a giant oak tree at age six.

Holding the boxes together was getting difficult.

Constant upkeep.

As he still fished for a solid thought, Dylan found his eyes wandering to the moving trees on the other side of the window wall.

It took a minute for Dylan's eyes to adjust but he could make out the dust particles dancing in the sunlight beaming in through the window, the kind of window with chicken wire buried in the glass. He watched the particles move and sway, forming shapes as he felt the all too familiar numbness of medication running through his body. It was a mix of peace and dizziness, all the while feeling like a heavy anchor. The problem, at least one problem, with living in a mental hospital (or 'psychiatric unit' as one of the 'nurses' insisted on calling it) was that you're left to your own devices for too long, and after a certain point, after been given the guided tour of the small ward, there is surprisingly little to do on the ward other than watch daytime soaps on the television or read month old magazines the 'nurses' brought in as an afterthought. All that is left is to adjust to living within the walls of the hospital and wonder what's going on on the outside, something Dylan found himself thinking of often.

There were four wards that made up St. John's Psychiatric Hospital, all named after species of bird: Raven (Crisis), Magpie (Senior Dementia), Petrel (Adolescence) and Crow (Minor Criminal).

Dylan had been placed on Raven ward which had thirteen bedrooms with their own private doorless wet rooms and toilets. Dylan was lucky and got room thirteen. At one end of the ward was the dining room, with its plastic forks and plates but surprisingly good food. Each night a 'nurse' would sit at each table and make sure the patients were eating. At the opposite end of the ward was the dayroom, where patients were encouraged to spend their time as being alone in your bedroom was considered unhealthy. The ward was at full capacity, all thirteen beds were filled.

Dylan had had time to watch the other patients but was still figuring them out. Most were older than him by ten or so years and he knew their names only by the small handwritten whiteboards on each patient's bedroom door: Aaron, Scott, Cathryn, Lara, Lewis, Sam, Paige, Damien, Adam, Charlotte, Marvin, Sue and Dylan himself. Though Dylan was unsure of their illnesses or disorders. Some were informal voluntary patients, others, like himself, were sectioned and forced to stay. Some screamed at the television, raving their thoughts were being stolen by the weatherman on the news. Others tried to lift the heavy furniture and throw it at invisible enemies. Others caused no trouble and clutched old teddy bears and mumbled to themselves, while others sat on their own crying for most of the day. Most patients were busy fighting their own battles and kept to themselves. Moods were unpredictable on the ward and Dylan knew he had to keep his defences up. Always stay on guard and never take his eyes off people. He had chosen the overstuffed armchair in the corner of the dayroom so he could see all those around him.

It was the sounds of the ward he had trouble getting used to. The shuffling of feet, the cries and moans, the yelling, the swearing, the frequent alarm that blared through the ward when there was danger whether it be a patient hurting themselves or, worse, others. The sounds all seemed hyperactive and hectic to the senses.

The people in his ears had retreated to the far side of his brain and they were all but a whisper. Dylan wondered if they might have some guidance for him but if he listened closely, he knew the 'nurses' would spot him and know he was hearing voices and force him to stay on the ward even longer, no doubt in a straitjacket in a padded isolation cell.

Atticus kept close to Dylan's feet. Ears low, eyes darting around, his tail like blurry smoke.

"Medication time," 'Rita' said as she walked around the patients, turning some by the shoulders toward the medication window in the middle of the ward.

Dylan didn't move. He simply watched the other patients make their way to the window where they lined up against the wall like a firing squad execution and waited for their pills or injections. It wasn't his time for medication. He was still reeling from the last dosage and knew there were no more pills until bedtime when Mirtazapine (an antidepressant, the witches told him) would knock him out cold and put him into a dreamless sleep.

For now, there was nothing to do but think. Dylan wanted to ask for some leave to walk the hospital grounds but under his section he wasn't allowed through any locked doors to the outside, and besides that he was also still on suicide watch; a 'nurse' checking though the little window in his bedroom door every fifteen minutes.

He wanted to see Cecilie, Maya and Henry but the emotions he felt when they came seemed to be smudged. It was his two best friends who had him sectioned in the first place as his next of kin. His parents had died many years ago and Dylan now lived, with his girlfriend Cecilie, in the spare room at Maya and Henry's house. It was comfortable and good to be around friends, somewhere safe and familiar. If perhaps they were younger, someone might mistake it for a student house, but the university is nearly twenty miles away. Dylan could only remember snippets and vague images of the night that got him to the hospital; The distorted hallucinations he had been so sure

31

and certain of, the kitchen knife, the blood on Henry's arm, a smashed window. There had been tears and screams, but he could not recall who from. All Dylan was aware of was the screams and cries echoed and haunted him.

Dylan thought of Cecilie and closed his eyes, falling into a medicated sleep.

***

"Dylan?"

He heard his name but didn't want to open his eyes. He hoped he would open them and be in his favourite chair back at the house. He prayed he would open his eyes and be somewhere kind and warm but as his mind caught up, Dylan remembered he was in Bedlam away from the sane.

"Dylan? Wake up. Medication time," the voice repeated.

Opening his eyes to the bright lights from the ceiling, the dazed patient looked up at the 'nurse' named 'Tom'.

"Nine o' clock. Time for your medication," said 'Tom'.

It was dark outside the windows. What felt like a quick cat nap turned into a seven-hour sleep, yet Dylan did not feel rested. His muscles were stiff and his limbs heavy. 'Tom' placed a firm hand on Dylan's shoulder, and they walked to the 'nurse's' station where 'Mandy' handed over a small paper cup with a capsule pill inside. As much as he wanted to decline and reject the poison, Dylan knew that would result in being restrained and a needle in the backside. In one quick movement, almost like a magician, Dylan tipped the pill into his mouth and immediately pushed it up under his upper lip and gulped the lukewarm water 'Tom' handed him. It tasted like chemicals. 'Mandy' inspected under the tongue and then nodded to 'Tom'.

"There we go, Dylan," 'Tom' said with a wicked smile. "There's a good quiz show on the TV if you want to watch that before bed?"

Dylan's thoughts were not on quiz shows. They were on timing. A very tricky task of timing. He couldn't help the medication they had injected him with upon his admission, those drugs were already whizzing around his system causing chaos, but the pills he had just 'taken' were in his control. He knew he couldn't go straight to the bathroom in his room and spit out the pill, the witches would know what he was up to. On the other hand, he couldn't wait too long, or the pill would start to break down and dissolve in his mouth and be absorbed into the bloodstream. They'd dull his senses and awareness. Anyone on the ward could be a witch. Anyone. Patient or 'Nurse'. Who knew what kind of witchcraft was happening within the hospital walls where no one would believe a madman.

He estimated he had ten minutes before the pill would break down.

Staring at the shadows on his bedroom wall, Dylan laid awake after refusing to take his optional sleeping pill. Perhaps it had been a mistake after the nap in the dayroom, but it was at night that the witches struck. His mind was too occupied with worries beyond his control. What if Earth ran out of water? What if a fire broke out in the forest around the town? What if witches were coming to kill him? The witches had been playing on his mind for days now. His frustration came from the simple fact that there was no way of knowing who was and who wasn't a witch . They hid in plain sight. It was a troubling dilemma. Suspect everyone until proven innocent.

The worries were torment and sleep did not come that night.

Autumn had quietly come across the town of Port Hampton over the last month. Darkness came in earlier every evening, casting long haunting shadows across the hospital grounds and now the season was in full swing. It had always been Dylan's favourite time of year. He loved the colours, the chill on the wind, the frequent drizzle of rain and the omnipresent smell of bonfires and pumpkins. This time of year had a warmness to it that wasn't present in any other season. It comforted him, especially in the very special month of October, which Dylan wished could be three hundred and sixty-five days long. The autumn shivers were a pleasure. Scarfs and mittens came out of the bottom drawer of the dresser, hot chocolates and tea replaced the ice-cold colas of summer, trees shed their leaves of red, brown and yellow, blanketing the whole town, wind whistled under doors and loose windows.

Being sectioned had robbed him of such pleasures.

A box opened on night fourteen in the hospital.

Memory had a funny way of coming to the front of Dylan's mind, almost like blooming spring flowers that uncurl and reveal themselves. Some memories are pleasant and others not so much.

Tonight, the memory was a good one from a time when his madness was just starting to rear its vile head...

Port Hampton had only one bookstore, 'Otter's'. It was on Castle Street, just next to 'Taylor's Hardware'. It was a quick walk from the house Dylan shared with Maya and Henry and it was a walk he made at least twice a week to pick up a new book. Books from every time and place that could be imagined. If one were to read for twenty-four hours a day, it would take three lifetimes to read all the books. The small shop, a former baker's, was a staple in the town and did well. New books in the front room where they were neatly arranged and displayed and in the back room were shelves full of all kinds of different second-hand books, once loved, discarded but now waiting for a new lover. The smell of the books, slightly like vanilla, sent the imagination running a mile a minute with different adventures and wonders. The mystery of what might be behind a tattered book cover fascinated Dylan to no end. Their combined knowledge was astounding.

Atticus led the way to the front desk.

Behind which sat a girl.

Cecilie.

It had been just over a year since Dylan had first laid eyes on her and he knew right away she was someone important. What simply started as simple hellos and goodbyes as he passed the front desk soon developed into questions about herself and how she was enjoying life in sleepy little Port Hampton. There was always a smile on her face, and she spoke in beautiful broken English. First Dylan had learnt little details; she was twenty-six, just a year younger than himself, she had moved to England the year before from Paris, she was learning English in the evenings by herself and every conversation between them showed improvement. Soon, as their friendship bloomed, she spoke of her life in Paris; the arts, the jazz, the literature. She was truly a bohemian from Paris's golden age. The more she answered, the more Dylan carefully filed her answers into the safest box within his mind; the Cecilie box, which was always kept well maintained as best he could. It was not long before visiting Cecilie became the main reason to visit the bookstore. Every day, Dylan, after working at the hardware store, came and sat with her while she worked and helped the readers find their books. They talked for hours about everything from films to typewriters. They connected over their shared love of Miles Davis and The Beatles, they both had fallen in love with the city of Los Angeles, having both stayed at the same hotel at different times, they had both lost their parents; Dylan's to cancer, Cecilie's in an auto accident and they both loved the work of Steinbeck.

Their talks meant the world to Dylan.

It was coming up on six months since they shared their first kiss and Dylan was truly in love with her as she was with him

As he approached the front desk, feeling the delicate buzz of excitement and contentment within him, he could see Cecilie was engrossed and beautiful as she read. The joy on her face as she looked up at him made him feel wanted in a way only she could.

37

"Bonjour, Dylan. How are you?"

Her voice. Her accent. A soothing drug.

That day, Cecilie was wearing a violet knee length dress with white tennis shoes and a black cardigan with the sleeves rolled to her elbows. A brown leather banded wristwatch was wrapped around her right wrist with the timepiece on the inside (just like Dylan wore his own watch). The blue grey of the clock's face matched the same vivid colour of her eyes. Her blonde hair was styled in the usual loose curls and kinks. She wore tortoise shell eyeglasses, round. Her make-up was subtle and simple.

Dylan took in all her details in a second.

With a smile of deep rouge lipstick, she kissed Dylan, holding it for just an extra second so it felt like their very first kiss, though there had been hundreds, if not thousands, over the last few months.

Rain struck the stained-glass front windows in a gentle, strange melody.

Interrupting his beautiful train of thought like a bulldozer was a different memory. One he would have rather forgotten or repressed.

Just as the toxic pain of panic spread through him, intent on overwhelming him, a stillness, unusual and unexpected, washed over him, like cooling air and silence filled his ears. He could no longer hear the cheers and calls of the other students, only see their mouths moving in silent words as they waited to be served at the busy student bar.

And then, like the slowly rising smoky wisp of an extinguished candle, they began.

> *Hello Dylan.*
> *Dylan!*
> *There are three of us.*
> *Remain silent.*
> *Or.*
> *We will kill everyone in this room.*
> *In.*
> *Cold.*
> *Blood.*

And then, they began to laugh.

The night 'nurse' peered through the little window in the door as she passed his room.

Dylan kept his eyes tightly closed trying to grasp that day and recover it in his memory. Thinking of Cecilie was getting him through the long nights. He turned in bed, wrapped in the cold, sweat soaked sheets and fought against the random thoughts coming to his mind.

He was in 'Otter's' again. He picked up the memory like a severed dream...

Running a finger across the spines on the shelf, Dylan wondered what book he would take home. The feeling of books under his fingers was a pleasure. Each book, much like its contents, was different. Some creased and dog-eared paperbacks, some were handsome leather editions from a different time, others were worn cloth bindings that had seen better days and then there were those books carefully wrapped in plastic to keep them safe. The choice was vast and entirely up to him.

For the last year, Dylan had been reading nothing but Cecilie's recommendations and not once had she chosen a bad book, if such a thing existed at all. Each of her books had its own charm and direction. No two were the same and each took him to a different place. It was books that gave Dylan some sort of stability during the last year. Books were a portable joy and innocence, something to keep in your coat pocket for when rain clouds came across the dark skies. To open to any page and read of some strange and magical world was a comfort that he relied on. It was not to say that they always worked. Some days the letters on the page became meshed together and unreadable like some alien alphabet but Cecilie helped during the times the books didn't.

"What are you in the mode for?" Cecilie asked, looking over the stack of books in her arm as she refiled.

Mode? Mood.

Dylan had gotten used to her broken English. It was something he found endearing. She was by no means unable to speak English but, rarely did a day go by where she wouldn't ask about a phrase or a word. His ears and mind had become so seamless at understanding her that it was often only upon reflection that he realised she had used the wrong word.

"Mood," Dylan corrected politely, just like she had asked him to do.

"Mood," Cecilie repeated quietly, and she nodded.

Yummy French whore!
Such lush tits and pussy!
She wants it all over her!

"I think maybe…" Dylan began, without knowing the end of his sentence.

"Science fiction?" she suggested. "Horror? I know you like horror."

He shook his head. He didn't want to read a nasty book.

"Err…let me think. I try and guess," she looked over the shelf before them, her eyes rapidly reading titles and spines. "Not fantasy, I know you don't like that. Historical maybe? A detective story? Oh no, I know…"

She smiled and with a raised slender finger pulled a small book from the shelf. It was a hardback, about the size of her delicate hand. Red cloth bound with a matching-coloured ribbon poking out through the faded gold leaf pages.

"Le Fantome de l' Opera," Cecilie said with perfect dictation that sounded elegant and romantic. "Gaston Leroux."

Dylan opened the small book to its title page and was relieved to see it was in English. He may have loved to hear Cecilie speak in her native language but beyond the basic French he learnt in school many years ago, he could neither speak nor read it.

"It is good mix of lots of genres. There is romance, horror, drama, mystery," she said.

"I think we have a book then," Dylan smiled.

"Another trip to Paris for you. I think you'll like it. Romantic, like you," Cecilie smiled, placing books back on the shelf. "I need to file these. I see you out front?"

He nodded and after a kiss to her cheek, he watched her disappear down an aisle. Now he was alone, he could hear the people in his ear stir. They spoke in quiet whispers, but they were awakening and trying to catch Dylan's attention.

Oh, that French slut!
I bet she sucks cock good!
Mmm…eat that wet cunt!

"You don't talk about Cecilie," Dylan was firm.

The people in his ear settled down to mysterious murmurs he couldn't make out. He was suspicious of their obedience and wondered if he was in for more trouble, but they remained quiet and hidden. It was rare he spoke back to them, for that was acknowledging them and letting himself be drawn into interacting with them, which never ended well. He stood still and listened closely, wanting to reassure himself that they were quiet and were, for once, listening to him.

Dylan was still and headed for the front desk followed by faithful Atticus.

Walking home, Dylan knew It was there.

It had an icy breath, scolding down his neck.

Its straw hands trying to wrap around his body and squeeze the life from him.

It was trying to fill his veins and arteries with hay and straw.

Its wide gaunt mouth expanded and contorted.

It screamed.

Atticus ran for cover in the wind-swept bushes.

Dylan was frightened.

Scarecrow.

At the edge of the grounds, there stood a large chain link fence with barbed wire on top. It was the only thing separating Dylan from the rest of the lucid world. Dylan let his eyes follow the road leading to the hospital gates. It led steeply down through a deep forest and then on into the town of Port Hampton, which was once Dylan's everything. He knew every street, alley, dirt road and path worn through the grass. He walked them daily, rain or shine. Always keeping himself busy and preoccupied. The only thing that remained relatively unchanged since his childhood was the charming quaintness of Castle Street. The street ran through the middle of the small town and although a lot of the major shops and restaurants had opened in the new shopping complex outside of town, there were still cafés and shops mixed with the thatched roofed cottages and antique lamp posts, which had been switched from gas light to the electric light so many years ago. The street's surface was a complex and beautiful puzzle of cobblestone which could be felt under foot through one's shoes. Each house and shop had graceful flowers hanging in baskets which brought colour to the almost sepia toned street. Shading the street from the warm sun were the giant horse chestnut trees, which in autumn, were a stunning deep maroon and mustard yellow. It looked, on some days with the right eyes, like a painting by some master painter.

It was peaceful.

It was pleasant.

It was safe.

Dylan had often wondered what caught his interest and mind so much about Castle Street but could never figure out a single reason. He had foggy memories somewhere in his mental library of days spent down the street with his mother, window shopping with an ice cream melting down his small arm and his mother buying him a new book on every shopping trip, usually a Stephen King novel. But, as much as he tried to clear the fog surrounding the boxes, he couldn't keep a firm grasp on them or even form a clear picture of his mother in his mind.

Dylan often wondered if he had a case of rose-tinted glasses, that he saw everything through a nostalgia filter.

The answer hardly mattered to him.

Day nineteen.

The coffee wasn't great in the hospital's canteen, but it was drinkable. Francis had decided to have a therapy session away from the office, somewhere where Dylan would feel more relaxed and calmer. The canteen was at least open and bright, and they had the large room almost to themselves as lunch finished an hour ago.

Francis sipped his vending machine latte and looked over the notebook in his hands, reading back over notes of past sessions while Dylan waited quietly wondering what would happen next. The doctor was taking great care figuring out the next session and its best direction. It made Dylan care about the doctor, that he was taking his time to think rather than bombarding Dylan with medications that would dull and fizzle his mind, leaving him out in the dark to cope on his own, unable to fight off witches.

Atticus snoozed on the table next to theirs. Dylan watched him with a slight smile. He was yet to tell Francis about the fox and hadn't even decided if he would or not. That could mean more pills and longer in hospital.

"I think we should take a look at C.B.T. How does that sound, Dylan?" Francis asked.

"Okay," Dylan replied, unsure what the abbreviation meant.

"So, we use C.B.T as a therapy at St. John's and a lot of people have said it has helped them massively in their recovery. I think it is AS important as medication, in fact. Cognitive

Behaviour Therapy is where we kind of take the links your brain makes, and we rewire them to link things differently. An example might be that when you get your low periods, the ones you tell me about, your mind might jump to more depressing thoughts and feelings that sink you deeper into your depression, but with C.B.T we can change those links. So maybe you take a precious thought, one you enjoy and find happiness with and conjure it up and go to that thought when you feel lonely and sad. So, do you think you have some kind memories you feel might make you happier?" Francis asked.

Dylan reached back into his boxes and searched himself. With the boxes fading, the management of the memories was difficult for him. What memories had been left untouched by his horrible illness? Which had been saved from their ultimate demise? A collection of boxes, the ones where Cecilie lived, were the strongest and most secure. They were the ones he tried best to keep untainted and untarnished. He thought back to the first time he saw her. When it had poured with rain and there was nothing to do but spend a day in the warmth of the bookstore. He had seen her sitting at the desk and was taken aback by her face. She had been wrapping new book arrivals in plastic backing to keep them safe. Her quiet ways impressed Dylan and he found himself stealing glances at her as he began to make up thoughts about her name and her past. When he heard her voice, it was like hearing music for the first time.

Dylan settled on the memory of that first meeting. "Yeah, I have one."

"Great. So, what you need to do, when you feel low or feel like a low period is coming on, I want you to grasp that special memory and hold it tight in your hands. You want to be able to look back at that memory and conjure up all the feelings of happiness and contentment and relive them. It should be a memory that you look back on with fondness," said Francis.

"Now, an extension of that is if we take those happy thoughts, we then take an object. Now, it could be anything. It could be a small soft toy or maybe a special wristwatch or something small and we link those happy thoughts and feelings to that object. In theory, and with practice, every time you pull that object out, the happy memories and thoughts will come back to you automatically. I think that would be a good idea for you to use."

The idea was a new one to Dylan. He thought about what he could use. There was a book in his pocket but not a special one. It would need to be something that already had significant meaning to him from the start. He settled on the thing he already carried around with him most places. A copy of 'Something Wicked This Way Comes' by Ray Bradbury, given to him for Christmas last year from Maya.

"We could try that," Dylan replied finally.

Atticus climbed off the table and like a house cat, sniffed at Dylan's feet then curled up and closed his eyes.

The hospital caretaker was mopping the floor on the other side of the canteen, but Dylan knew there was witchcraft involved. Her slender fingers scraped against the mop and her teeth were sharp fangs ready to draw blood. Dark eyes watched the patient and doctor.

Dylan felt the familiar sting of fear on the back of his neck.

"Maybe...maybe I could use a book?" Dylan stuttered, trying to focus on Francis.

"That would be an excellent idea, Dylan."

The caretaker looked over and smiled. Innocent to those who didn't know the truth about Port Hampton witches, but Dylan knew better. They hid in plain sight while people walked by unaware of the danger. That was the fear, they were nearly undetectable.

"Are you okay?" Francis asked, concerned.

Looking over at Atticus, who gave a single nod as

confirmation, Dylan paused and considered his words. What he was about to say could result in more time locked up in the madhouse. This was a great fear, but he trusted Francis. He wasn't like the other doctors and nurses.

"Do you believe in witches, Francis?"

"Witches? Like, broomsticks and black cats?"

"Like, witches that do horrible things."

Francis rubbed his chin. "I…well, there are people who follow the Wicca religion. Some may call them witches."

"I…I think Port Hampton is haunted by witches."

Silence.

"Do you often fear witches?" the doctor asked.

Dylan nodded once, his eyes still on the witch with the mop and evil intentions.

"What do you think they're doing?" Francis made a note.

"I think they want to hurt people…because they were executed. Do you know about the trials?"

"Well, if I can remember my school days…The Port Hampton witch trials of sixteen-ninety lasted seven months and ended with twenty executions at the castle. The bodies are buried somewhere there in an unmarked mass grave," Francis explained, thinking back to his younger days. "But, that's history, Dylan. It was a long time ago and just brings the tourists to Port Hampton."

"I think…. they want revenge."

"Do you think they want to hurt you?" asked Francis.

"Yes." Dylan confirmed.

Silence.

Atticus growled at the witch.

"Are there witches here?"

The caretaker was coming closer, her bloody mop in her hand and her eyes screaming violence. She had a blank face, a face of no feeling or consciousness. Dylan's heart raced and a

cold sweat beaded on his forehead.
    She was coming for him.
    To kill him in the open because he knew.
    He knew they were trying to get revenge.
    What warped plans did they have for the town?
    Would they burn everyone alive and breed more witches?
    "They want to kill me," Dylan wept.

Night had come again. Wind beat at the window.

The bedsheets were sharp and coarse and the air in the room was thick with suffering.

It had been several hours since he had turned off the light but there was no sleep. Dylan clung to the hope that sleep would come if he simply lay silently in bed in the dark, but it had eluded him. His tears were all too real and stung his hot cheeks. The thoughts of execution chambers and three steel boxes buried in strange purple soil somewhere in a place he had never seen but couldn't stop thinking about. The thoughts were stuck on a permanent loop, over and over again the same two thoughts. Though he tried, his mind would not empty or deviate from the same two thoughts. Trying to push them away only brought them back to the front of his mind and they were unavoidable. No war, personal problem or anxiety was more important than those boxes in the purple soil and macabre execution chambers, where men died in the darkness of a black hood.

Who would find the boxes? Someone needed to find them.

They were too important to ignore.

How could he possibly sleep while they were hidden in the purple soil? He felt guilt and worry.

All night, his mind warped and tangled, never forgetting those same two thoughts

Day twenty-three.

The bright wind through the slightly opened window had a sad minor note if Dylan's ears were correct.

"Should we do our rating system on the worry chart?" Francis asked, while he drew a long line on a piece of paper then started numbering underneath the line. One to ten. He turned the notebook to face Dylan and with the tip of his pen, he pointed to the digits. "So, here at number one means you're feeling very low and unhappy. Then at this end, number ten, is feeling very happy and really good about yourself. Where do you think you are this week?"

Looking down at the page, Dylan found himself feeling profoundly stupid. The symbols Francis had drawn looked like foreign hieroglyphics, completely alien to the things he had learnt in preschool. It was a prime example of his mind emptying, a thing that was happening more and more frequently since last Christmas. He knew he should remember what the symbols were, even a four-year old would know but, he found himself lost for an answer. He knew one end was good and one end was bad. Left side, very unhappy, right side, very happy.

Gripping the pen Francis handed him, Dylan circled the middle of the line and looked up at his doctor to make sure he had done the right thing.

"So, a six, not good but not bad either. The same as last week, isn't it," Francis observed. "And what about your anxiety levels?"

Dylan circled closer to the left, the very unhappy side.

"So, a four. That's a bit lower than last week, down from five. Why do you think that is?" asked Francis.

> *Keep your fuckin' mouth shut!*
> *We'll choke you while you sleep!*
> *He's getting inside your head!*

Dylan knew the truth but was afraid to say, afraid to acknowledge it. He tried his best to deny it.

Francis waited for an answer.

Finally, after mustering his courage and bringing it to the tip of his tongue, Dylan muttered so quietly he could barely hear himself or be sure in his own unstable mind or that he had even spoken the words out loud.

"Pardon?" Francis strained to hear.

"The scarecrow," The words felt cold in Dylan's mouth.

Francis made a note. "You mentioned the scarecrow in our first session. When did you see it last?"

"This morning, at breakfast...I think it was stalking me," Dylan confessed as he fidgeted in his seat with the burning urge to stand and shake all his limbs and scream at the top of his lungs, but the feeling subsided as quickly as it reared its ugly head.

"We're yet to talk in depth about your hallucinations, as you say you haven't been ready," Francis commented.

Dylan shook his head.

"Do you want to discuss them a bit now?" the doctor asked.

The quiet came over the room again as Dylan turned thoughts over in his head. He tried to keep them in their boxes, but he was having difficulties. His thoughts were like liquid being poured from a jug, gushing and splashing and never settling. They were impossible to grab and hold onto.

Francis made another note.

Atticus circled the room and sniffed at the doctor as if confirming who it was. The fox bowed its head in approval.

What was he writing? Something horrible no doubt. Insane, lunatic, madman? Surely not Francis.

Dylan's inner voices roared.

He wants to lock you up forever!
You're a fuckin' madman!
He'll give you a lobotomy!

After a long moment of thought, Dylan replied. "We can."

The beetles were, thankfully, on the outside today. The lower half of the window wall was black with masses of bugs. Their bulbous bodies scraping together like rough sandpaper and sounding just as unpleasant. Their clicking pincers dripping with a toxic venom waiting to make the victim catatonic with a single bite.

Never turn your back on the bugs, Dylan told himself.

"Where do you want to start?" asked Francis.

"The scarecrow," said Dylan, trying to hide the fear in his voice.

The beetles were bad but at least Dylan could see them. It felt safer talking about the scarecrow while it wasn't there.

"You want to talk about the scarecrow?" Francis clarified.

Dylan nodded once.

"Can you describe it?"

"I don't know if I can…"

Francis rubbed his beard and thought. "What about drawing it? Do you think that might be easier?"

He leant forward and handed over his notebook. Dylan was certainly no artist but in his mind's eye, he tried his best to allow himself to picture the thing that tormented him.

The pen touched the page and he began to sketch.

Big, very big.

A tatty black suit.

Hands and feet made of straw.

A burlap sack head.

Torn mouth spewing multi legged crawling beasts.

Dark, hollow eyes.

Red mist cloud.

"Does it have a name?" the doctor asked.

Dylan shook his head. Just scarecrow, and nothing more.

"Does it talk to you, Dylan?"

"No."

The monster made chilling sounds that Dylan was unsure he could put into words, and he was also unsure if the noise was heard anywhere else in the world.

Dark.

Hollow eyes.

Bigger.

Deeper.

The biggest fear, the one Dylan felt rising in his throat, was the worry that he had opened the chest full of mental disease and he would never be able to put the lid back. Like a ruptured sewer pipe spewing all kinds of filth and illness that were simply too powerful to contain like a violent animal.

Darker eyes.

"How often do you see it, Dylan?"

Dylan couldn't make the eyes dark enough or hollow enough. Those eyes were like craters, drawing the scarecrow's victims in with its mindless gaze, drawing them in to suffer.

"Dylan?" a distant voice said.

It's coming for you, cunt!

Darker eyes.

It's going to kill you!
Sick eyes.
Fear the scarecrow!

Dangerous eyes.

The paper ripped under the pressure of the pen and the scarecrow's face became a torn mess. Exhaling deeply, Dylan pushed the notebook across his lap. He wasn't ready. He knew he had made a mistake. The regret was painful and made him feel sick in the head and stomach.

Now it was just a matter of time.

It would come soon. He knew it would.

"I can't...I'm sorry..." Dylan muttered.

The smile again from Francis, like a smile from an old friend. "That's okay, we're not going to push anything. We're just here to talk."

Francis took back the notebook and turned to a fresh page.

"Atticus," Dylan said, looking at the fox sitting nearby.

"Sorry, Dylan?"

"There's a fox. I see a fox...but he's hurt. He has an arrow through his head and a bloody face. He doesn't seem to mind it but...I don't know," Dylan explained as Atticus watched a bird through the window wall. "He's kind of nice and doesn't bother me."

"Would you say that it's a good thing to see?" Francis asked.

"I...I guess so. He's a little like having a pet. He moves like a strobe light and...well, I don't know how to explain but he sometimes looks like smoke."

Francis wrote down a thought. "I would take that as a win then. Some people who have your illness see nice things and they don't bother them. They simply accept it and move on with their lives. That's what I plan to help you do, Dylan. We want you to move on with your life and not let these hallucinations bother you to the point where you can't function normally."

"Bugs," Dylan said quietly.

"Bugs?"

"Bugs."

56

"What kind of bugs, Dylan?"

The window wall was still swarming with seemingly millions, so many Dylan couldn't tell him how many varieties there were. Crawling up the glass and over each other. It was as if they were trying to get into the room...trying to get to Dylan.

Dylan pointed a finger which the doctor followed with his eyes. "Beetles, spiders, cockroaches. I think...I never know if they're real or not."

"What makes you think they're not real?" asked Francis, leaning forward.

"People...people say they're not real and not there. Sometimes I see them, but other people say there's nothing there...so they can't be real."

"I can assure you there are no creepy crawlies here," Francis said calmly.

"But how do I know they're not real if there's no one else around? I seem to see them more and more when I'm alone with no help," Dylan sighed.

"That's a good insight, Dylan. So, if others say there aren't any bugs, then you realise you must be hallucinating. Is that right? Do you believe that you're hallucinating?"

"Sometimes," Dylan replied after a pause.

"So, to some degree, you realise you're seeing something that isn't there," Francis paused, clearing his throat. "See, I don't want to use the word 'real'. Some say 'real' is a relative term. Now, someone without schizophrenia wouldn't see what you're seeing but that doesn't make it any less real for you. It's still a real fear for you. It's as real as everyone else's and I can imagine you get very anxious when you see these bugs."

"I hate them...I can't breathe, and I shake, then breathing gets hard. The panic hurts my chest," Dylan cried.

He let his eyes fall back to the window. There was no sign of the bugs. Not even a cobweb. They were gone.

"A logical thought we might have is, say the hospital was indeed crawling with bugs, we would call an exterminator if there was such a problem, wouldn't we?"

The logic was sound, but Dylan didn't see how it applied to him.

"So, many times when you see these things, the unpleasant things, we could try asking ourselves what other people might do."

Dylan could feel his mind wandering but tried his best to keep a grip on the conversation.

"We've discussed that, typically but not always, symptoms are brought on by stress," said Francis. "Stress acts as a trigger."

"I don't really feel stressed," Dylan explained unsure. "No more than usual."

"You may not know you are though," Francis countered.

This puzzled Dylan. "What do you mean?"

"What I mean is the subconscious mind, YOUR subconscious mind, may be stressed. There might be an underlying threat or anxiety causing you stress, but you haven't uncovered it yet. Of course, seeing and hearing what you do is very stressful no doubt, but there might be something else." Francis theorised.

Dylan nodded quietly. "Maybe it's the thing...I worry about."

"You mean the problem we discussed during our first few sessions?" asked the kind doctor.

"Yes."

The Scarecrow is coming, Dylan!
It will eat your flesh!
We'll kill you before it does!

"But...I don't know if I should..." Dylan said, feeling the uncertainty in his chest.

"Why's that?"

They came like a wall of sound, wailing from different places deep within him. The people in his ear screamed of despair, anger and pure hatred.

The witches were out hunting for him...they curled their bony fingers and cast hexes to try and find him. What would they do with him? He was frightened by images of bubbling cauldrons in a cave in the shadow of Port Hampton castle. They were all standing around, chanting a strange and bizarre language...spells against the townspeople. They flew across the moon on their brooms, hoping to catch him sleeping so they could take his mind and make him do horrible and vile things.

Dylan cried himself to sleep.

The alarm cut through Dylan's peaceful dream like a chainsaw, ruining a kind memory of a summer day in the back garden with his friends where there were no locked doors or chicken wire windows. Cecilie had been there. Henry had been working on the barbeque and Maya was making gin and tonics. It had been a beautiful relief, but he quickly came to the conclusion where he was.

Atticus perked his ears and eyed the door.

In his half dazed, half medicated state, Dylan shuffled to the door and peered out of the observation window.

There was commotion in the room next door. Adam's room. 'Nurses' hurried past and were shouting over the screeching of the alarm.

Something bad had happened.

Francis came into view. He had a pale, blank face with a deep look of shock and pain.

His shirt and hands were streaked scarlet.

Blood.

After what seemed like an hour, though in fact couldn't have been more than twenty seconds, the alarm stopped, and the commotion died down.

***

The patients of Raven ward had been gathered in the dayroom the next morning. Some of them were weeping quietly, others were outright bawling their eyes out and some remained silent waiting to hear what Dr. Grierson had to say. It was the first time that Dylan could recall seeing all the patients in one room at the same time. The only person missing was Adam and though it had not been said yet, Dylan knew why.

Dr. Grierson explained in a slow tone, which to Dylan's ears sounded condescending as if he were talking to a group of five-year-olds, that Adam, during the night, had taken his own life. He would not elaborate how but Dylan had the distinct idea that it had not been a peaceful suicide. Judging by the blood on Francis's hands and shirt. It had been violent, painful and lonely and Dylan was left with a hollow feeling in his stomach wondering if it was he who would be next.

The witches would come for him soon.

Dylan tried to think of something happy as he sat in front of the television with unfocused eyes.

The dinner at the restaurant had been wonderful and now, in the heavy drizzle of falling rain, Dylan and Cecilie made their way down Castle Street hand in hand. The loud tap of rain gave their walk rhythm as it hit the umbrella they shared. They kicked their feet in the puddles as they walked, and it was not long before Cecilie was jumping into them with both feet. The puddle exploded with giant water drops flying into the air and falling back down with the rain.

Cecilie pointed at the puddle in front of Dylan. "Jump!"

After a slight hesitation and over thinking, he leapt both feet into his puddle. The muddy water sprayed up onto his jeans, making little Rorschach tests.

A simple and pure glee filled him which peaked every time he landed in a puddle. How many times had he done this in the first ten years of his life and taken it for granted?

The simple joys.

At this time of day, it was only him and Cecilie on the street. No cars, no other people.

The rain had cleansed the town of troubles and sin.

The town was pure again.

Day twenty-five.

Dylan and Francis stood in the middle of the room. The dark rain poured in a thick curtain outside, denying the patient a view of nature. The doctor looked at Dylan with mournful eyes.

"Take a seat, Dylan, and we'll begin," Francis said softly. "I think it's important we talk about the news we had this morning."

"Adam killed himself," said Dylan softly.

"Unfortunately, yes. I'm sorry to say. I…" began Francis.

"Last night, he was laughing and seemed fine," Dylan observed.

"Well, that's the thing. We can all SEEM fine but it's sometimes painful feelings and thoughts that people hide. They wear this mask that shows the whole world they're fine but in actuality…they're not okay," Francis explained. "I can't go into details, obviously, but I think that Adam wore that mask."

Some dark thoughts crossed Dylan's mind. How had Adam ended his life? Hanging? Sliced wrists? Overdose on stashed medication? It was not something they were told so their only comfort was imagining that Adam did not suffer.

"Are you okay then, Dylan?" Francis asked. "Let's talk about you."

Dylan knew that would be all the talk there would be about Adam. A tragedy quickly wrapped up and dealt with. Francis was clearly saddened.

"Sometimes it's difficult. You know, telling the difference."

"Difference between what's real and what's not?"

Dylan nodded.

"Is there anything I can help with?" Francis offered, opening his notebook.

Dylan knew it was Francis' job to care and he was doing all he could, except the patronising part of it all. It made Dylan like him more.

"Maybe," said Dylan.

"Just let me know how," Francis smiled wearily.

Dylan shook his head. "I feel old sometimes."

Dylan knew he had changed the conversation drastically, but it felt like the right thing to say. His train of thought worked in strange ways.

"Old?" Francis repeated. "But you're only twenty-seven. I wish I was that age again."

"There are people younger than me, and they've done so much. So many great things and I don't feel like I've done anything. None of my goals have been reached."

"You want to leave your mark on the world?" Francis asked.

"Why else live?"

Atticus wandered the room, bright burning eyes scanning the room, his tail low to the floor and crimson blood dripping from his facial wound. Dylan hoped the fox was okay

"What about your stories? They've been published. People will find them. Being a published writer at twenty-seven is an amazing achievement. Maybe you could get them published in a short story collection or something."

Dylan counted. He had eighty-three short stories (six of which had been published in magazines) and a third draft of a novel written. Some good, some bad, most fell somewhere in the middle he felt.

"I suppose...but they're not grand 'I was here' statements. I can barely seem to remember when I wasn't ill. My writing is the only thing I could think of that would be my way of leaving a mark. My only way of saying I was here. I worry about how much has been lost because of this sickness. Friends and people drift away and lose touch and soon you find there's no one to turn to," Dylan said, wringing his hands. "Have you ever had a plan? Like a plan in your head. Kind of like 'at this age, I'll be here' and then 'at this age, I'll be there', that sort of thing? Planning out your life. But then it doesn't turn out that way because something gets in the way and throws the train off the tracks, and you're forced to take another rail. Something derailed me and it's not fair."

Dylan took a deep breath. It hurt to reveal so much.

Francis sat silent, considering his words. "I imagine a lot of people with your condition feel the same way."

"Doesn't make it any easier," Dylan said bluntly. "Has your life turned out the way you thought it would?"

"I don't know. I'm a clinical psychiatrist and that's what I wanted to be. So, I suppose to some degree, but I never planned on getting divorced at twenty-nine. I never planned on losing my parents at thirty. I had a very rough few years. But things work out in their own way, at least I like to imagine," Francis explained. "But you know…I suppose, it comes down to one thing."

"What thing?"

"Well, are you a destination person or a journey person?"

Dylan thought. "I don't know. What's the difference?"

"Okay, so when you have a goal, whatever that goal might be, do you find it's just about getting to that goal and the journey is just something you have to do? Or do you think the journey is what you enjoy more rather than achieving the actual goal?"

"Hmm…I've never thought about it like that before."

"So, which are you, Dylan?"

66

Blank. Suddenly. His mind was nothing but blank.

"Pardon?" Dylan asked, feeling shaken.

"What kind of person are you?"

"Which person?"

"When you have a goal…." Francis began.

"I don't remember," Dylan replied flatly. "I don't remember."

"Are you okay?" Francis asked with concern.

"Sorry, I don't…I don't remember what we were saying." Dylan felt embarrassed. He knew it was the witches stealing his thoughts.

Concerned, Francis sat forward, closer to his patient. "We were talking about being a destination person or a journey person. Do you remember?"

Dylan felt his mind going into a frenzy as he tried to remember. "No…"

"I was saying that some people think a goal is the main thing and…" Francis began.

The sudden recollection struck Dylan like an electric shock straight to the brain…like the dreaded electric shock therapy they did in some dark room in some hidden corner of the hospital away from the eyes of authority.

"Yes! I remember!" Dylan yelped suddenly, feeling the relief of memory.

"That's it, yes! Well done," Francis clapped his hands together. "Good, good. So, which do you think you are?"

"It depends on how the journey is. If it's rough or smooth. Long or short. Painful or peaceful," Dylan theorised. "Do you think mental illness is a journey?"

"That's an interesting notion," said Francis, with a scratch of his beard.

"It's a tough journey," sighed Dylan.

"I bet," Francis paused. "I'd like to try and understand more though."

"What do you want to know?" Dylan asked.

"I'd like to understand schizophrenia from someone who suffers from it. I want to hear what it's like from someone who deals with it day to day."

"Don't you read enough of that in books? Surely, I'm not the only schizophrenic you've talked to," said Dylan, eyeing the sleeping fox at his feet. A friend but a true sign of madness.

"I've read a lot of books, yes, and I have sat in on other doctors talking to schizophrenics, but you are my first assigned patient. The first one completely under my care," said Francis. "Adam was my second."

"Oh," said Dylan. He felt an odd sense of purpose being Francis's first assigned patient. He felt like he had a use.

"And yes, there's books about the illness, but they're views from the outside. They're views on how things SHOULD feel and they're assumptions based on statistics. What I think I find in you, Dylan, is that you're incredibly insightful."

"Oh…"

"So, I want to know how it feels, not just what you see and hear," Francis said.

After taking a quiet moment to arrange his thoughts and weighing his trust in his doctor, Dylan replied slowly. "Tired. Worn down. Isolated…alone. Those are pretty suitable words, I suppose. Like, it feels like I'll never be normal. I'm scared of my own thoughts. The idea of being alone at night with my head running through horrible things makes me sweat."

"That sounds terrible. Do you feel alone often?"

Dylan thought of Cecilie, Maya and Henry. "I have people who help me, close friends…and you of course."

"Do you have many friends?"

"I used to have lots of friends. We all used to go drinking at university and would hang out and play games and talk but you know, after I got ill, people dropped away. People don't want to be with a crazy guy. Soon, I just stopped getting invites to things and I stopped hearing from people."

Francis began to talk but Dylan knew the floodgates were open and there were still things left to say. He spoke slowly as he carefully tried to explain it as clearly as he could. "I fear…. that maybe my mind will keep slipping away piece by piece and I'll get worse and worse. I've seen older people with schizophrenia and how they've turned out. I worry, worry so much I can't sleep some nights, that I've seen my future and I don't want it. Dylan is better than that. I try to be normal but it's not so easy to act normal. It's more like a pressure to feel and act normal. Like, that's what everyone else does so why can't Dylan? I spend a long time getting my head straight then I'm thrown into complete chaos. Kind of like a little rowboat on a stormy ocean. People say to ignore it, but they assume it's crazy thoughts, but it makes complete sense. It just makes sense, and I can't separate or figure out the strange thoughts from normal thoughts. There is no red flag or warning that it's a crazy thought. It just makes complete sense."

Atticus barked and growled at something unseen at first, then Dylan noticed the beetles coming into the office under the door, like water.

"From what I can gather, chaos is a very appropriate word," observed Francis.

The flow through the floodgates was a strong current, there was no stopping the reel of subconscious pouring out. "It's a very strange feeling knowing you're a hostage to your own mind and medication. Sometimes the people in my ear force me to do things and threaten to bring out scary hallucinations like spiders or something…I get worked up and I never know what a day will be like. It could be nasty and scary in the morning, or it could be calm. I hate the unpredictability of it all. I try very hard to prepare myself for each day but it's like barely grasping onto my sanity with just my fingertips. Always just in reach but always slipping. A storm on the outside can sometimes be a nice thing. I quite like it when it rains heavily and there's thunder and lightning and you're all warm and safe inside with a good book."

"But you're talking about a storm on the inside?" The doctor made a note.

"Yes…on the inside sometimes I can't keep a thought straight in my head and I get wound up, tight like a clock spring. I can't keep myself calm or in one place. Everything becomes panic. I become very…I don't know the word. Wound up is the best way to describe it. I get very uncomfortable with myself. It makes me want to be…"

> *You fuckin' nutter!*
> *You're worthless!*
> *Why can't you be normal?*

He shook his head, trying to still the people in his ear.

"Want to do what?" Francis pressed.

"Makes me want to be dead," Dylan said quietly.

Francis took a fragile breath. "Do you think of death often?"

"Depends."

"On what?"

"I never think of hurting other people. I could never live with the horrible guilt if I ever hurt someone. That's too horrible to imagine," Dylan thought of the blood on Henry's arm that night.

"But what about hurting yourself? Do your storms happen often?" asked Francis, concerned.

"Everyday."

"Are you still taking your medication?"

The wind was loud, and Dylan felt cold.

The fox barked at the ever-growing mound of beetles and Dylan remained silent.

A box tumbled open.

The people in his ear had been raging all day and he had finally succumbed to them. He had been drawn into a screaming match that echoed through the rooms of the bookstore. Cecilie had come running, tears forming in her eyes, and she watched him argue with phantoms unseen.

He hated himself for being pulled in, but the situation had reached its breaking point.

Cecilie took him by the shoulders and turned him to face her. She looked sad but brave. She spoke in quiet whispers, assuring Dylan it was okay. Each one of her words brought the people in his ear down and buried them back into his subconscious. Her drug suppressed all sounds within him. She sat with him for hours, practising the breathing exercises he had been told by his doctor and reading from the nearest book she could grab. It was something for Dylan to focus on, something for him to follow and breathe to.

He was thankful for her.

He sat cross legged on his bed, the only sound was his laboured breathing and the pounding patter of rain on the window. The everlasting storm had not ceased and didn't look like it would anytime soon. He was thinking about Cecilie. He could remember her sweet perfume and the sound of her keys jangling as she locked up the bookstore. Dylan waited at the bottom of the stone steps, feeling uneasy as the night approached. The darkness was always a fear of his, never sure what might be lurking out there. It was a fear of a three-year-old not a twenty-seven-year-old. It made him feel like a baby.

"All locked. Can you put in my bag?" Cecilie asked, turning her back to Dylan.

He did as she asked and they began to walk down Castle Street, hand in hand with the cold on their faces. It was peaceful moments like this that Dylan loved and cherished. The simple pleasures gave Dylan the biggest reward.

"What would you like to do tomorrow?" Dylan asked.

"I have writing to finish," Cecilie replied with a smile. It was a surprise to hear.

"What are you writing?"

"It's about…Well, I don't know yet," Cecilie said. "I started but find I cannot tell where story is going until I get there. It flows. Is that the right word?"

Dylan nodded. "Yes. I find some stories work like that too. I try and plan it, but it doesn't always pan out."

They walked in silence, enjoying each other's company and

warm hands.

"I am inspired by you," Cecilie squeezed Dylan's hand gently.

"By me?"

"I think your writing is brave and el-owe-gant," Cecilie pronounced. "I want to write stories like you."

She held tight to his arm as they turned onto Proctor Street.

He could remember their trip to the zoo. He clung to the happy memory as flashes of lightning illuminated the room.

The train rattled down the rails, cutting through the bright and green woodlands around Port Hampton. The sun beamed brightly through the windows, giving the train a warm glow.

In the woodland clearing, they saw a mother deer and her fawns.

"Oh, look, a family!" Cecilie said gleefully.

Dylan couldn't help but smile as he watched them play in the low bushes, chasing each other's tails. Their innocence and carefree existence made him happy. How different he felt away from town with Cecilie next to him, leaving all his troubles behind at the train station, even just for a day.

Calm and serenity. Nothing to fear or worry about.

Free.

More lightning and thunder seemed to rattle both the hospital and Dylan's mind in the darkness of the room.

Through the glass wall, in the clear blue water, Humboldt penguins swam in zigzags, darting in all directions, catching their fish lunch in their beaks. Their movements fascinated Dylan, who thought they reminded him of dancers in tuxedos or maybe circus clowns.

"They are like clowns," Cecilie giggled, raising her camera to take a photograph.

The sharp prick of panic hit Dylan's chest. Had Cecilie just read his mind? She wouldn't do something like that, not to him…would she? No! Of course not. Cecilie was wonderful to him and certainly wouldn't betray him. The two of them had simply thought the same thing and that made him smile, a rare piece of logical thinking. The ease of communication and understanding was exhilarating. Something cosy and familiar to a broken mind.

The penguins danced in the water. Atticus sniffed at animals and followed the couple like a faithful dog, cocking his head at the animal's calls and roars. It was a busy day at the zoo. Families pushing prams and children stood on tiptoes over the fences to see animals lounging in the bright sunlight.

It had been Cecilie's idea to come and Dylan was very happy to be out and have, just for a day, a feeling of complete contentment wash over him.

That was a good day. Cecilie had asked several times, in the kindest way, how he was doing. Never prodding or jabbing him for an answer. Cecilie knew full well about his troubles and had a way of putting Dylan at complete ease.

She was a kind and beautiful soul.

And that day, as they saw zebras, rhinos, cheetahs, lions and a whole ark of other animals, the people in his ear did not utter a single word.

Day twenty-seven.

He awoke at three in the morning from a dream. Not a sudden cold sweat wake up from a bad dream but a silent slow wake, that severed the dream from his consciousness. He had been with Cecilie. He had dreamt of fixing fences in their garden, reading the Sunday newspaper over coffee in the morning, writing his fifth novel in the upstairs office while Cecilie and their young daughter played joyfully in the living room, sending laughter and giggles up the stairs to his ear where there were no people.

Their own quiet, peaceful house. Together.

Starting at five-past three in the morning, Dylan sat at his desk with a pen and fresh paper and for five hours, he wrote a story about a book clerk with a passion for life and literature. Every pen stroke was done with care and consideration. When it came to the title page, as the morning sun filtered through the bars across the windows, he thought of his dream and wrote;

'For Cecilie by Dylan Samuel'

Don't you tell the cunt!
Shut your fuckin' mouth!
You're sick! Nothing but sick thinking in a sick mind!
Get your cock out and show him!
Choke him with it!

Sweat began to bead on Dylan's forehead and the back of his neck. He tried to talk but felt icy inside, cold and hard. Images of dark horrible shapes raping Francis stabbed at the front of his mind. Hateful visions that repulsed Dylan. His eyes were wired open by the witches, and he was forced to watch. There was no fleeing.

"Are your voices telling you not to talk to me, Dylan?" Francis asked, unaware of the vile shapes.

The doctor's once safe office was now a dark, horrid place.

The room was silent.

"Do you feel scared of them?" the doctor asked.

Dylan mumbled quietly. "Please make them stop."

"Dylan?"

He began to cry. "Please make them stop."

Francis leant forward and placed a caring hand on his crying friend. "I'm working on it. WE'RE working on it."

"I just get...I get...they call me horrible names. They call me..." choked Dylan.

Francis gave a trusting look. Now, Dylan had seen many looks over the last few months but there was no judgement in the room today.

There was help.

Dylan spoke in a hushed whisper, making sure only Francis would be able to hear. These were not words he wanted anyone else to hear. "They call me...call me a paedophile...and a rapist...or a deviant. They call me bad things."

Without missing a beat, Francis began to speak. "I can tell you now, I know for a fact, a full-fledged fact, that you are NOT a bad person. You are not a bad person and certainly not those horrible things they call you. I promise you that."

Rape the children!
Fill 'em with your cum!
They're your playthings!

Looking down at his hands in agitation, Dylan knew he had to say it, to say it to himself out loud. "I'm not a bad person...I have NEVER looked at children like that or women or anyone. Never. I'm not a monster," Dylan tried to keep his voice steady. He had never wanted to make himself so clear in his entire life. "They...the people in my ear...they say such horrible things, vile things. They make me feel guilty and ashamed. How do I separate normal thoughts about...S...E...X and the things they say? I don't want them to mix up. Dylan isn't a bad person, but he worries one day...what if the people in my ear turn me into something horrible? What if they can control my mind and make me do vile things? I'm scared."

You want to fuck babies!
Stretch out their assholes!
Rip them wide and eat them!

Tears flowed as Dylan's heart raced, pounding in his chest. His sweat soaked through his shirt. "I don't want to be a bad person. Dylan ISN'T a bad person. I'd rather die than become what they call me. Dylan is a good person."

He felt Francis' hand on his shoulder, gentle hands holding him still. "Hey hey, Dylan it's okay. Calm down, it's okay."

The doctor was soothing. They both stood for a moment while Dylan tried to catch his breath and hold back the floods of tears. He couldn't remember standing up from his chair.

"You're okay Dylan. It's all okay, don't worry," Francis assured. "A lot of other people with schizophrenia have similar troubles about sex. Be it thoughts of child abuse or sexual assault but, and I cannot stress this enough, they are strictly involuntary. They are not your own thoughts. These nasty thoughts are based on a fear you have of becoming horrible. Your illness is unfortunately using your fears against you. They are NOT your own thoughts. It's almost like the horrible thoughts have been randomly inserted into your mind. Now, don't take me literally, people can't put thoughts into other people's heads but, the human brain, and especially this disorder, can work in very strange ways and can sometimes do these bizarre things. But the important thing is that these unpleasant thoughts are completely involuntary. A lot of people who suffer the same disorder have these bad thoughts. However, the simple matter is that these intrusive thoughts disgust you, they make you feel sick as you've said before. You neither enjoy nor like them. Well, that is a hundred percent proof that you are not what you fear so much. It makes you completely opposite to the thing you fear."

Dylan nodded slowly, just grasping the concept.

"Unfortunately, the voices you hear say such nasty things, constantly repeating them, so it's understandable you might start feeling those false doubts and thinking you may become something bad. But there is proof that the thoughts repulse you and you don't want them."

"No, not at all."

"Do you think actual paedophiles and rapists feel bad about the thoughts they have or the crimes they commit?" Francis asked frankly.

"No."

"There's your proof. The thoughts, again not your own, repulse you."

"I'd rather kill myself than become one of them," Dylan replied with full honesty.

Francis made a note and the room fell silent. Even the people in Dylan's ear were reduced to a slight murmur. "We might need to up your medication, if you're still having severe hallucinations like you describe. You're on Amisulpride?"

"Yes," Dylan lied. It had been a month since he had taken any medication voluntarily. They wreaked havoc on his mind and body. They made him sluggish and dull, and Dylan knew he needed to stay sharp and alert to keep away the witches.

Francis made another note. "I have to ask you about your risk levels. Have you had any thoughts of harming other people?"

"Not at all." And that was the truth.

"And what about harming yourself?"

Dylan dropped his gaze to the floor. "Sometimes."

"What kind of thoughts do you have?"

"Lots of thoughts."

Francis made another note. "Are they the sort of thoughts that come and go like quick flashes of lightning or do they tend to linger and hang around?"

Dylan pondered. "Dylan doesn't know."

"Do you realise you keep referring to yourself in the third person, Dylan?" Francis questioned.

"Do I?"

"Yes, and several times in the session you've done it. Another common symptom of schizophrenia," Francis explained.

"Oh."

"Do you do it often? Refer to yourself like that? Like 'Dylan is walking in the park today' or 'Dylan is making dinner'."

"I don't know, sorry."

"That's okay," Francis smiled. "I know it's hard to open up and tell people things, but I feel I can really help you. So far, you've been really good at explaining yourself, with impressive insight, a rare thing in schizophrenia. If we can keep up this rhythm, then hopefully we'll be able to continue on a solid road to mental recovery and we can release you from the hospital."

The room became heavy and cold in an instant, full of echoes reaching deep into the corners of the room. The hair on the back of Dylan's neck prickled and sweat dripped from his armpits. The cold was seeping through his shirt and into his very bones.

Chilling.

Sharp.

Painful.

The scarecrow stood in the corner. Its long slender arms twisted and reached out from its side, engulfing the walls around it like a cancer, coming closer to Dylan. The long straw claw like fingers extending out, reaching for him. Parasitic worms looking for a host. The red and black spiders falling from the torn abyss of its mouth. The groan that came from the contorted sack face brought instant tears to Dylan's eyes. The blood red mist surrounded it.

Horrific and frightening.

Dylan closed his eyes tight. Do your counting, he told himself.

One... two... three... breathe deeply... don't open... your... eyes... yet... one... two... three...one... three... two... two.... one... two... three... one... two... one... please be gone... one... two... three... please God be... gone... one... two... three... one... two... three...

Dylan held his breath and gathered his courage.

Be brave.

He opened his eyes.

The scarecrow was gone.

The red mist that seeped from its eyes lingered in the air.

Francis was looking at him with concern.

The doctor's wristwatch beeped. An alarm.

"We've come to the end of today's session, Dylan," Francis explained, still looking at Dylan for signs of distress and torment. "You're making astounding progress. We need to sort out our next session, but I think if we can keep this up, you will make an excellent recovery."

For the first time in a month, Dylan had been granted an unsupervised walk of the hospital grounds. He was finally allowed out of locked doors and could enjoy the illusion of freedom.

He had wrapped up warm in his bathrobe and put on his slip-on shoes (he was still not allowed shoelaces) and walked down the stone path between the recreation hall and the dormitories. There was the sound of birds and a wind that felt nice on his ears and neck.

Atticus jumped and chased butterflies as they moved from slowly dying flower to flower. He made a noise that made Dylan feel happy for his friend. The fox seemed at peace and unaffected by the fact they were still locked up in a madhouse.

Dylan, on the other hand, was very aware of the fact as he couldn't escape it. The time in the hospital was beginning to get to him and now with Adam's suicide, Dylan feared it would not be long before the witches made him do it too. He knew it was the witches that got to Adam. They had killed him or at least made him bleed and die. Dylan had no doubt about it.

It was while Dylan thought of protecting himself that Atticus found the bin. Up against the high fence, a large rubbish bin had been placed.

Atticus had jumped onto the bin.

Down here by the edge of the grounds, no one could see him. It was a blind spot. A flaw in the hospital's security.

The fox barked once at Dylan and jumped over the fence

into the trees and sat, waiting for Dylan.

If you don't fuckin' leave, the witches will get you!
Fuck this place!
Get out while you still can!
The witches will kill you like Adam!
They'll murder you!
This is a place of death!
Run!

Dylan did not hesitate.

He jumped onto the bin, with a quick look around the grounds. No one was there. Gripping the wire of the fence, Dylan wondered if it was the right thing to do but the people in his ear were persuasive and he knew that witches were just waiting to catch him with his guard down. He raised himself up and over and caught his leg on the barb wire at the top of the fence.

It would be the only blood he would spill in the hospital.

Atticus barked and ran into the woods.

Dylan followed and disappeared amongst the trees.

Dark.

Darkness and nothing more.

The woods scraped and cut his flesh.

Port Hampton.

Witches.

Trials and executions.

They were tortured.

Flew on brooms at night.

Appearing before people as spectres.

Finger pointing.

Hysteria.

Paranoia.

Witchcraft.

The woods were dark. Problems muted together and used their cracked skulls to move things together. What could he do? Wait? Wait for them to find him? Wait for them to rip his blood and flesh. Satan's children. The Devil had come to Port Hampton. Deeply affected with soul preservation. What's in the big dark house? Were they there? Hiding…plotting…plotting their revenge. Dead babies split from genitals to mouth, dripping with blood. Horrific sights, never ceasing and never flinching. The fog churned here. Fog still flowed through tiny cracks. Witches made him crazy. It was spreading. The hysteria. Eaten and burnt alive. They were the ones. The cogs drilled into the walls and burnt the floor, scorching the wood. Rip the scum from the earth. Surely, they'd strangle and choke the life from him. The gears jammed. It was speeding up and couldn't be stopped.

Blood on the brain. It screamed like razor blades on a soft throat. What if you were afflicted? What then? You become accused and then killed, hung by the neck by angry people. The machinery churned and blew smoke from holes on each side. Saturating the brain and slicing through thoughts and connections.

Cunt!
Faggot!
They're coming.
You'll fuckin' die!
Rot and seep into the ground.
Fuck your babies!
Kill them and tear them apart!
That's what witches do!
The witches are coming!
For you!
To bewitch you.
Take over your soul!
Chain you down!
Destroy people.
Kill them.
Murder their children!
You'll burn!
Suicide!
Do it!

Nothing more, unable to see, the ground, the woods were a dark and dangerous place, lost with nothing to help.

Where was he? The dark house. Lane at the end. Decomposing. Scarecrow. Made of straw. The brain died and was kept in a coffin. Dark and dank. Rupertic. Franlic. Katzne. Scared. Keep the code: 9876789 He wanted Cecilie. He wished Adam were alive to help. Lost in translation. Broken connection.

Fuhim. Kelmo. The gauntlet of psychosis. His face on a lamppost. 5-11, Missing. Mis-crossed wires. Brain damage. Burning kerosene. A fox in the foliage. Teeth breaking on the ashes and ripping gums from the skull. Where was this dungeon? Where was the window? Air! Lungs needed filling. Reaching up into the darkness, clawing, scrapping, cutting. Witches were coming.

The scarecrow morphed out the tall, dense trees.

It howled and screamed a death rattle.

Atticus lowered his ears and bared his teeth.

The red mist seeped from the scarecrows' burlap sack head.

The fox jumped and roared at the monster with the straw hands.

Dylan cried and tried to run.

Atticus fought a brave fight, ripping straw from the monster's feet and arms.

The scarecrow fled into the darkness.

Atticus had won.

And out of the depth, he cried. "Help Me."

Dark.

It had begun to rain heavily as Dylan stood outside the house that Atticus had led him to.

The fox had led him home.

Cold and confused, with a mind that could barely stay on a train of thought, Dylan looked up and saw his friend Maya in the upper window. She was a sight for sore eyes, and he felt glad to be home. He wanted to yell out to her but felt he had lost his voice. Was it the right decision to come home? He wasn't sure but it had been Atticus who had brought him here and he trusted the fox.

The front door swung open, and Henry came out carrying a box of recycling to the curb. He was quick off the porch and down the front steps, trying to stay dry from the downpour.

He tipped the box into a bin and in a quick glance over his shoulder, his eyes found Dylan.

"Dylan?"

And Dylan stepped forward into the glow of the yellow streetlight.

"Dylan, is that you? God! Please come here. Get out of the rain!" Henry called, jogging across the street. He wrapped his arms around his friend. The embrace was a great comfort to Dylan. "Come on, buddy. Let's go in."

***

Maya had brewed the coffee, but Henry handed Dylan a

cold beer and Henry clinked his bottle with Dylan's. The clock in the living room struck two in the morning and the room was silent except the beating of the rain on the windows and roof.

Dylan had dried off with the towel Maya had given him and his soaked and ripped bathrobe was hanging on the warm radiator. Maya sat under a blanket with a look of worry on her face. Dylan was yet to say a word and he was worrying that he had terrified his friends turning up in the middle of the night.

It was Henry, always the voice of logic and reason in their friendship, who spoke first. "How are your arms?" he asked, looking at the thin, bloody cuts on Dylan's arm. Wounds from the forest.

Dylan simply nodded, not feeling their pain.

"Dylan, we're really glad to see you," Maya smiled, putting a hand on his leg. "Really. We're happy to see you. We tried to come visit but they said you weren't allowed visitors at the time. Henry nearly yelled at those doctors trying to get a visit but..."

"It's true buddy, we tried. But...so you're here now...the hospital is going to be worried about you," said Henry.

Dylan finally said something. "Atticus led me here..."

"He's always been a good fox, huh?" Henry smiled, looking at his fiancé Maya with a look of concern.

"Do you think you're okay? I can see a lot of blood."

"I'm fine," Dylan said quietly. "My friend died."

"Who, Dylan?" Maya asked, sitting forward.

"My friend Adam. He killed himself. The err...the witches killed him, and I didn't want that to happen to me...but...I don't know. Atticus led me home. That has to mean something...right?" Dylan mumbled, staring at the wet fox huddled in the corner.

"I think..." Henry said slowly. "You know, Dylan, we love you and we just want to see you get better..."

"But...a hospital is so horrible...they're dark places," Dylan looked at his friend with teary eyes.

"But...you know. Do you think that maybe the doctors are there to help you? I mean...do you have even one doctor you like?" Maya asked.

"I..." Dylan thought of Francis and felt the wave of guilt that came with knowing Francis would be angry and ashamed of Dylan leaving the hospital. "I think my doctor won't be happy. He was kind to me...and like a scared kid...I ran."

"Dylan, I don't doubt you were scared. I mean, I've never been to a psych ward, but I don't think I could manage what you have had to deal with for the last...what, nine months? I have no doubt you've been through hell. But there are things that can help you," Henry said, then took a long sip of beer.

Dylan could sense there was genuine love in the room. Maya and Henry were his best friends, and he knew they had his best interests at heart, but how could he go back to the hospital knowing what had happened to Adam? He tossed these thoughts around his mind as he watched a tear roll down Maya's cheek.

"I just want you to be well. So does Henry and Cecilie. I mean, your doctor. Dr. Romero, he's been telling us you're making great progress. We just want you well, Dylan. We love you so much and can't bear to see you like this...so..." Maya couldn't finish her sentence.

"I think Dylan, based on what Dr. Romero has told us. That you're getting better. Better than he really expected, and you can't give up now. You're so close to getting a grasp of this," Henry said with a hand on Dylan's damp shoulder.

"I think you have all the weapons to fight this, you know; pills, therapy, us, Dr. Romero...you just...I don't know, need a push to keep at it. You know you're always welcome here. You'll always have a home with us, no doubt, and we'll be here waiting for you, but I think you need to go back..."

The thought of going back hurt Dylan but the look on

Henry's face and the pain in Maya's eyes hurt more and told him it would be the right thing to do.

There was a knock on the front door. Maya stood, tossing the blanket to one side.

"That's Cecilie," Maya said to Dylan. "She's worried for you and wants to know you're okay. Do you want to see her?"

Dylan was speechless. He felt indescribable guilt and shame having escaped a mental hospital and been a burden on his friends.

"I do," Dylan said in a clear voice. He wanted nothing more.

Dylan stood and passed Maya to get to the door.

Outside, Cecilie, soaked to the bone and with tears in her eyes, beautiful and like the final key Dylan needed, looked wide eyed at Dylan and threw her arms around him. They held each other tightly in the downpour.

Dylan had never loved her more.

It was the next morning, October 31st, Halloween, when Francis came to visit Dylan in his room on Raven ward.

The doctor sat on the edge of the bed. Dylan held the leather notebook Cecilie had given him last night in his hand. He ran his finger ever so gently over her elegant handwriting:

'For Dylan' by Cecilie Sauveuse

"How are you finding the medication?" The doctor asked, after hellos and handshakes.

"There's a lot of stuff zipping around," Dylan replied glumly.

"The side effects should wear off after a couple of weeks, it just takes a while for medication to build up again, especially new ones."

"I don't want to be here but..." Dylan hesitated.

Francis leaned forward. "You can be honest with me."

"They're here to help me."

"That's right. The doctors here do care about you and want to see you get better."

"So, I take my pills and do the therapy....and hope I will be better by the end of the twenty-eight days, or at least well enough to function properly," said Dylan, rubbing his hands nervously.

"We can arrange for other types of help for you when you leave here; cognitive therapy, group work, a social worker..." Francis listed.

"Weapons to fight my battle," Dylan's new mantra. "Will you

be there?"

"Yes, of course."

"Promise?"

Francis thought. "How about this, you promise me that you'll keep up with the medication every day here and outside the hospital, and I promise I'll do everything in my power to stay assigned to your care as long as you need me."

Dylan considered it, then held out a hand. "Deal."

They shook hands.

The journey had begun.

The fox at Dylan's feet curled up his orange tail, closed his bright eyes and slept.

Dylan kept his promise to Francis and took medication every day during his section at St. John's Psychiatric Hospital.

Including the anti-nausea and sleeping medication, the total was four hundred and fifty-one pills.

Four hundred and fifty-one.

451.

AFTERWORD

Asylum, Madhouse, Looney Bin, Funny Farm.
(May 28th, 2022)

There are lots of names for the place where I currently am. To the uneducated public, the mere words 'Mental Hospital' stir up images from horror movies of forced Electro-Shock Therapy, straightjackets and padded cells for dangerous people who should be locked away for the rest of their lives. It fills their minds with all kinds of fears, misconceptions and false realities...of course, on the other side of the coin, so does Schizophrenia.

It's my birthday in a couple of days, I'll be thirty-two and I am due to stay on the ward for the next week at least. At first, the thought horrified me, but I've come to learn since arriving here that, despite my inner demons, delusions and hallucinations, people are here to help me and keep me safe from my own worst enemy: my mind.

It's a long journey.

I will keep this afterword short as I believe the novel does a better job of explaining this devastating disorder and hopefully it has helped you, the reader, to understand Schizophrenia and hospitalisation.

I wrote this novel through a filter of mental illness, through the good highs and the terrifying lows and I've tried to describe these thoughts, emotions and waking nightmares the best I can.

Dylan Samuel is Juno Jakob and Juno Jakob is Dylan Samuel.

There really is an Atticus and he sits currently at my feet while I write this.

We all find our guardian angels at some point in life, and they save us from the depths of madness.

Mine is a fox named Atticus.

And I am rising from the depths.

Juno Jakob
Bedroom 13
Hawthorn Ward
St. James Psychiatric Hospital
Portsmouth, U.K

9 781916 395398